Mom and Dad Don't Live Together Anymore

Christine Harder Tangvald
Illustrated by Benton Mahan

Chariot Books
David C Cook Publishing Co

Dedicated: To my dedicated editors—
  Catherine Davis, Julie Smith, and
  LoraBeth Norton.
Their expertise and hard work have produced
  many life-changing books for children.
God bless them, all three.

Chariot Books is an imprint of David C. Cook Publishing Co.

David C. Cook Publishing Co., Elgin, Illinois 60120
David C. Cook Publishing Co., Weston, Ontario

MOM AND DAD DON'T LIVE TOGETHER ANYMORE
© 1988 by Christine Harder Tangvald for text and Benton Mahan for illustrations.

Cover and interior design by Dawn Lauck

First Printing, 1988
Printed in Singapore
93 92 91 90 89 88   5 4 3 2 1

Library of Congress Cataloging-in-Publication Data

Tangvald, Christine Harder
  Mom and Dad don't live together anymore.
  (Please help me, God)
  1. Children of divorced parents—United States—Juvenile literature. 2. Divorce—Religious aspects—Christianity—Juvenile literature. I. Mahan, Ben. II. Title. III. Series: Tangvald, Christine Harder. Please help me, God.
HQ777.5.T36 1988   306.8'9   87-34211
ISBN 1-55513-502-1

Some families are happy, and there is a lot of fun and laughter.

But some families are unhappy, and there is a lot of fighting and crying.

It's not good for a family to be unhappy for a long time.

So, when a family has been very, *very* unhappy for a long, *long* time, sometimes the mother and father decide to get a divorce.

They just do!

Lots of families get divorced.

Some kids I know whose parents got divorced are:

1. _____

2. _____

3. _____

Divorce is something that is decided between a mother and a father.

Divorce means that the mother and father don't want to be married to each other anymore, and that they cannot live together in the same home.

Sometimes, then, the kids have TWO HOMES instead of one—one with Mom, and one with Dad.

One thing I *know* is that divorce is not the kids' fault!

Sometimes children think parents get divorced because the kids did something wrong. That is not the reason my parents are getting a divorce. It has nothing to do with me being good or bad.

People get divorced because they are unhappy with *each other*.

Sometimes I wish my mom and dad could be happy with each other again.

But they just can't. They said they tried and tried.

But I know my mom and dad are still happy with *me*!

Another thing I know is I AM LOVED!

Some kids have *both* a mother and father who really, really love them.

Some kids have a mother *or* a father who really, really loves them.

And most all kids have some other special people who love them, like:

A grandparent or

friend or

aunt and uncle or

brothers and sisters or

_____.

Some people who love *me* are:

1. _____
2. _____
3. _____

I know GOD loves me all the time. God loves me every single minute of every single day. He really, really does.

God even said, "Never will I leave you; never will I forsake you." (Hebrews 13:5b, NIV)

It feels good to *know* I am loved.

And I still love my mom, and I still love my dad. It's OK to love my mom, and it's OK to love my dad—even if they aren't together.

Some ways I can show my mom I love her are:
1. Tell her so.
2. Give her HUGS!
3. Draw her a beautiful picture.
4. Write her an "I love you" letter.
5. _____ .
6. _____ .

Some ways I can show my dad I love him are:
1. Tell him so.
2. Give him squeezes.
3. Draw him a picture of ME.
4. Send him a letter at work.
5. _____ .
6. _____ .

Sometimes my feelings get all mixed up. I feel like crying and crying. Crying makes me feel better— sometimes. It's OK to feel sad and to cry. In fact, it is OK to feel however I feel.

Here are some feelings other kids have had when their parents got a divorce:

relieved

sad

lonely

embarrassed

unhappy

Do you ever have any of these feelings? It's OK to be *upset* during a divorce. That's just normal.

Another thing that is normal is for feelings to go UP and DOWN and UP and DOWN.

angry

guilty

confused

afraid

But it's not good to get sadder and sadder, and madder and madder.

And guess what! Some kids whose parents get divorced feel RELIEVED! It's true. Not all the time, but sometimes.

Because now maybe the fighting and crying will stop, and the parents can be happy again. Lots of families are happier *after* a divorce.

They really are. And I know I will be happy again, too.

Yesterday I felt _____ .

Right now I feel _____ and

_____ .

Tomorrow I hope I will feel _____

_____ .

Sometimes during a divorce people say or do things that hurt other people.

You see, people are not perfect. Mothers are not perfect. Fathers are not perfect. And kids are not perfect.

But God *forgives* people who aren't perfect. God forgives mothers. God forgives fathers. And God forgives kids.

Isn't that great?

And if God can forgive people when they hurt each other, then we can forgive, too. But forgiving is hard and sometimes it takes a long time.

Something I can try to forgive is _____

_____ .

I feel better when I forgive, even though it is hard to do.

The Bible says, "Be kind and compassionate to one another, forgiving each other, just as in Christ God forgave you." (Ephesians 4:32, NIV)

One thing that makes me feel better is to SHARE my feelings. It helps to *talk* to someone who cares.

I can talk to:

1. God
2. My teacher
3. My mom or dad
4. My best friend
5. My brother or sister

6. My pastor
7. A counselor
8. My dog
9. _____

Three people I will talk to are:

1. _____

2. _____

3. _____

Once in a while I just need to be all by myself to think and think and think.

If there is something I want to know about, I can ask QUESTIONS!

1. Will we be moving?
2. Who will I live with?

3. Can I still _____?

4. _____?

One question I want to ask my MOM is _____

_____?

One question I want to ask my DAD is _____

_____?

There are lots of other things that make me feel better, too.

I *love* to play with my friends. We like to run races and to _____ .

If I get *angry* I can kick a ball really hard, or pound a pillow, or _____ . But I do not hurt other people when I get mad.

If I get *sad* I can talk to Grandma or Grandpa, or visit a friend, or I can _____ .

It is even OK to cry.

If I get *lonely* I can cuddle with my favorite stuffed toy or blanket, or write a letter, or _____ .

And I can look in the mirror and SMILE at the person who is smiling at ME!

Another thing I can do is to TELL what is *important* to me. It is OK for me to say how I feel.

Things I can say to my mom are:
1. I love you, Mom.
2. Please don't say bad things about my dad.
3. God loves you and God loves me and God loves Dad.
4. Something extra special about you is _____ _____ .
5. One IMPORTANT thing I want to TELL my mom is _____ _____ .

Things I can say to my dad are:
1. I love you, Dad.
2. Please don't say bad things about my mom.
3. God loves you and God loves me and God loves Mom.
4. Something extra special about you is _____ _____ _____ .
5. One IMPORTANT thing I want to TELL my dad is _____ _____ .

One of the most IMPORTANT things I can do is to TALK TO GOD. God listens, God understands, and God cares.

The Bible says: "The Lord is my helper; I will not be afraid." (Hebrews 13:6, NIV)

I can pray, "Please help me, God, to understand things and to feel better."

One question I want to *ask* God is _____.

Something important I want to *tell* God is _____

_____.

It is important to ask questions and tell how I feel.

And I can have *good* times right in the middle of
hard times.

Yes, I can!

Here are some *nice* things that happened to
me today:

1. _____ .

2. _____ .

3. _____ .

Here are some *nice* things that I am looking
forward to next week:

1. _____ .

2. _____ .

3. _____ .

Next month we might even _____ .
Doesn't that sound like fun?

Here are some things about ME that are *special.*
1. I still have *lots* of friends!
2. I can still _____.
3. And I am really _____.

4. What I like *best* about me is _____.
   Here is a picture of *me* smiling!

Here is a picture of *me* running . . . fast!

My favorite game is _____.

My favorite food is _____.

My favorite place is _____.
   Yes, I can have HAPPY TIMES even if my parents are getting a divorce.

After a divorce, some kids have TWO HOMES—
one with Mom and one with Dad. And some things
change, but some things stay the same.

	MOM'S PLACE	DAD'S PLACE
My bedtime is:	_____	_____
Some rules are:	1. _____	1. _____
	2. _____	2. _____
	3. _____	3. _____
Things I keep here are:	1. Toothbrush	1. Toothbrush
	2. Pajamas	2. Pajamas
	3. _____	3. _____
	4. _____	4. _____
One thing I *can* do is:	_____	_____
One thing I *cannot* do is:	_____	_____

THINGS I TAKE BACK
AND FORTH ARE:

1. Suitcase

2. Telephone
   numbers

3. Stuffed
   animal

4. My favorite
   book

5. _____

6. _____

Here are some things *I know*:

1. Is the divorce my fault?

    NO, the divorce is not my fault.

2. Did I do anything bad to cause the divorce?

    NO, I did not. Kids don't cause divorce.

3. Do I have to take sides?

    NO, I do not have to take sides. I can love my mom and I can love my dad even if they are not together.

4. Can I do anything to get my parents to change their minds and get married again?

    NO, I cannot change how my parents are or how they feel about each other. I cannot stop the divorce, and I cannot make my parents get married again. That's just the way it is!

1. Is it OK to feel sad and confused and even mad?

    YES, it is OK to feel however I feel, even relieved.

2. Will someone always take care of me?

    YES, someone will take care of me—ALWAYS.

3. Can my parents take care of themselves?

    YES, I don't have to take care of my mom or dad. I can help, but I am still a kid.

4. Are _____ still my aunt and uncle?

    Are _____ still my cousins?

    YES, they are.

5. Will God help us through this hard time?

    YES, He will. God loves me and is always with me.

6. Will I be happy again?

    YES, I will. It might not be easy, but sometime later I will be very happy again. I can have happy times right in the middle of hard times, too.

Just knowing all these things helps. In fact, I'm feeling better already.

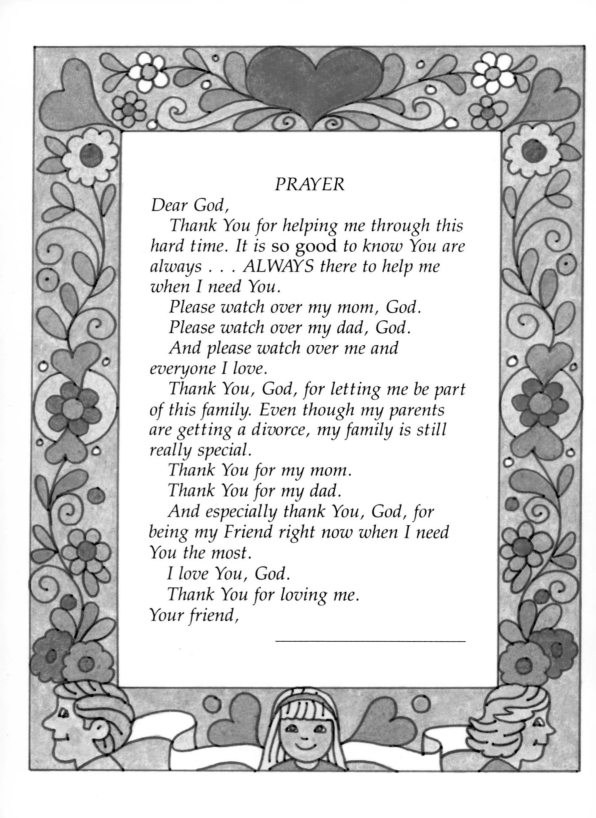

PRAYER

Dear God,

Thank You for helping me through this hard time. It is so good to know You are always . . . ALWAYS there to help me when I need You.

Please watch over my mom, God.

Please watch over my dad, God.

And please watch over me and everyone I love.

Thank You, God, for letting me be part of this family. Even though my parents are getting a divorce, my family is still really special.

Thank You for my mom.

Thank You for my dad.

And especially thank You, God, for being my Friend right now when I need You the most.

I love You, God.

Thank You for loving me.

Your friend,

_____

Jesus Christ is the same yesterday and today and forever. (Hebrews 13:8, NIV)

TEN SUGGESTIONS FOR PARENTS

1. **Unconditional Love**
   Through words and actions, show your child that you love him just the way he is.

2. **Physical Reassurance**
   Another important way to say, "I love you" is to hug your child, tuck him into bed, wink at him, comb his hair, hold hands.

3. **Keep Explanations Honest and Simple**
   Clearly and honestly state what is happening, but avoid blame.

4. **Keep a Familiar Routine and Set Limits**
   As much as possible, adhere to a familiar schedule. Also, establish and maintain certain limits. This provides a sense of continuity for your child.

5. **Positive Self-Image**
   Try to place your child in situations of success. Give each child a small bit of exclusive time and attention.

6. **Allow Honest Emotions and Feelings**
   Feelings need to be acknowledged and expressed. Three good ways to express them are: Say them out loud; write them down; draw a picture.

7. **Keep the Child Out of the Middle**
   Don't make your child choose sides or use him as a weapon, a spy, or a message carrier. Respect the rules in the child's other home.

8. **Use Positive Language**
   Try to use positive words of confidence, dignity, and self-respect.

9. **Good Physical Health**
   Take good care of yourself and your children. Eat well. Exercise. Get enough sleep.

10. **Plant Hope for the Future**
    Plan some enjoyable "right now" activities for yourself and your children, as well as something pleasant for the future.

Though divorce is often a difficult and traumatic transition from one period in your life to another, it is also a new beginning. Trust God to walk forward with you, step-by-step, into a hopeful and confident future.
God bless.

Christine Harder Tangvald

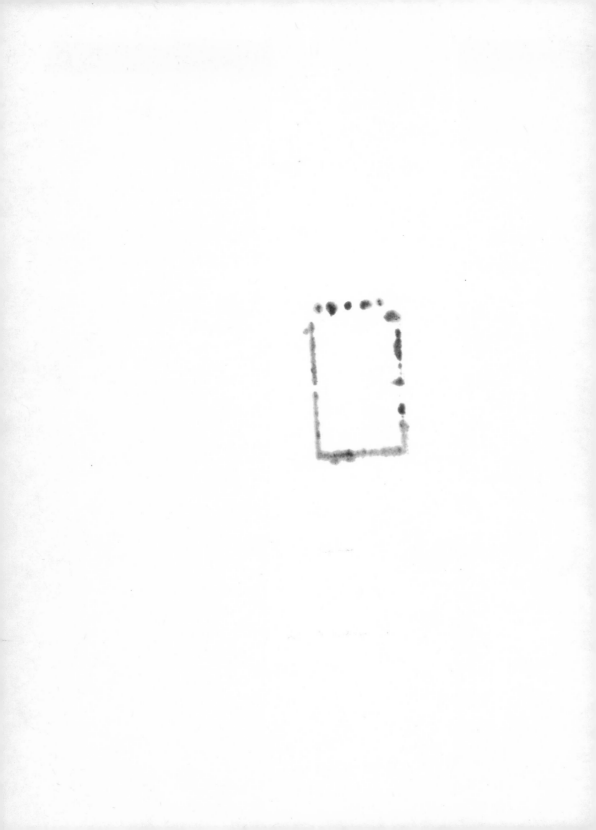